AKS HUCKLEBERRY

MAGNOLIA WINE

Imprint

Publisher:
Snap Collective
Is a trademark of
Rock N Books Ltd.
59 St. Martin's Lane, Suite 8, London, WC2N 4JS, UK

Printed at: EsserDruck Solutions GmbH Untere Sonnenstraße 5, 84030 Ergolding

ISBN: 978-1-914569-77-7

Design by: Tea Jagodic

To all the girls in my family,
blood and chosen, scattered all over the world.

Aksinia

What would you imply to blossoming?
Blossom me up... mmm
Thinking about what spring does to cherry trees…
I guess it could mean giving life, thus giving birth, impregnating.
Not my case for now.

However,
what I would imply is to wake me up, to let the spring fill my heart and soul again…
And my mind...
Oh, be my inspiration, blow my mind, blossom me up.
Oh please love me, and take care of me.

You, my adventure. You, my secret. You, my discovery...

I'm so fragile and tender in your arms,
teach me to love you, learn to love me.
Be my lover, I am so cold without you.

I'll be your blossoming magnolia.

Foreword by Natalia Lazareva

Imagine a gorgeous sunny morning, that does not begin helter-skelter, but lazily, without a hurry or any unnecessary ruffle. You wake up peacefully, and maybe even happy, and you open your eyes because you've had enough sleep rather than were rudely disturbed by an alarm… The light around you is speckled with gold and you are you. You then get up and go to the bathroom, where in the mirror you see yourself, your true Self : relaxed, confident, recipient to this world and listening with every fibre of your being, knowing, loving and appreciating yourself. Without masks, without any theatrical make up to hide behind, in a sacred union with that day and life around you.

Stories that Aks tells us through her artwork are about such moments. These are difficult to put into words and, I imagine, even harder to catch in their true essence. It is about a certain harmony between intimacy, an unsteady nature of each fleeting moment, honesty and secrecy. That is why each portrait is soulful and unique.

Introduction by Libby Symons

I have known Aks for over ten years now. She has grown and changed and faltered and thrived and questioned herself consistently throughout this time. She is always changing, moving, but her work captures a whimsy and a yearning that I find beautiful and strong. It is a consistent hunt for home. A blunt point of view through a beautiful and soft lens.

I've seen her work change with her environment, she takes and finds what feels like home in each space and explores it. She does this honestly and does not shy away from the complexities of that, the loneliness and isolation alongside the beauty and companionship. She looks for love in all of these places and often finds it with lens in hand. I would think that doing this is something that is often difficult and yet she remains open.

I remember her persuading myself and two actors to visit a beach in the middle of December – we are dressed in black, it is bitingly cold and we are covered in glitter willingly dancing on the pebbles, - such is the fantasy of Aks' world. In the past she has wrapped me in duvets, covered my face with petals and numerous times told me directly and simply that I did not look like myself yet. She was of course correct. I have seen my own face in ways I'd never considered because Aks saw something there. Therefore, working with her you learn an incredible amount. It is a unique experience where if you are lucky enough you will be let in to her world and learn her language. I think you can see this in her work too. People, nature, and home and the large complexities of all these things. They are all things that are solid and strong and consistent whilst incredibly fragile, pretty and ever changing. They are often sad. They are always beautiful.

Delicate, mature and unshaken, her photographs show her point of view. Her work will always be personal and her touch will always be delicate. I could not say the above without mentioning her strength, her strict viewpoint. It is what makes her work so interesting to me, that these tender moments in life can be so hard just as in life that is often the case, they can be inaccessible. So, in the face of this, she shows us her beautiful world and we are lucky enough to see it.

Introduction by the artist

I used to despise and to be terrified of being a woman. "Boys had it easy!" – I thought. No periods to suffer through, no patriarchal oppression. Back then, I used to not know what to do with men, how to photograph them, how to see them. So I turned to the most obvious but complicated subject for an artist – a Woman.

I started photographing when I was basically still a child, 14 years old, and, as mature of a child as I always was, I didn't know much of a life back then. I never kissed anyone, I never made love, and most importantly, I didn't fully know what it was really like to be a woman.

What I did feel in my heart even then, and what only grew now that I have been doing this for over 10 years, is the deepest love for women around me, the fullest admiration for a female body, strength and spirit, that I always tried to translate through my visual work. I found my muses in the most unusual and the most mundane of places. Occasionally, I would work with professional models, but the majority of gorgeous creatures in this book are just wonderful "normal" women - the girls of my family, my dear friends, strangers… Sisters from all over the world. Each of them opened up in front of my camera like a beautiful moon flower, shyly and slowly at times, while some passionately and readily, in turn making me blush. My little sisters grew up right in front of me, becoming strong magnificent women of extraordinary beauty, and I was lucky enough to witness this growth & capture it through my work.

I always knew I wanted to make books, fabulous intricate works of art, filled with images and memories and touching words, but it took me a while to figure out how I wanted to begin my published journey. The theme of my first book is the sacred nature of the Woman. I wish for whoever chooses to have this art object in front of them, to be filled with the beauty that is bursting out from my heart, to see these women the way I see them.

If you are patient and attentive enough, you might notice how my work has evolved through time, how from being innocent it moved into a more sensual realm, but remained gentle and deeply respectful to my subjects.

While the majority of these portraits have been taken in the last 3 years, I feel that this book will act as a beautiful closing chapter of all of my work up until now, where I am now consciously discovering womanhood for each woman separately and filtering it through my own view of a woman's essence and sexuality, translating it into new works of art.

The book ends with the latest series of nudes, which signify for me the beginning of a new journey – that of a wild woman, with a raw expression of her emotions, running through the woods with her wolves or, perhaps, swimming naked in the cold waters of the ocean. A woman, who is not afraid to be seen and heard.

My darling girls… Thank you for being so brave & never questioning me in my artistic process. You hid in any beautiful bush I admired, climbed any tree, ignored the stinging nettle in the fields and forests, had fake rose thorns glued to your spine, danced in the sun like no one was watching, posed in the snowstorm pretending to be warm, had petals attached all over each part of your bodies, laid underneath kilograms of cold clementines, had your first and last cigarettes, undressed for the first time for the sake of art, had real baking flour in your hair and liters of hairspray, survived 3 am call times & mosquitoes biting your yonis. You trusted me to photograph you even when you didn't like to be photographed by anyone else.

Some of these girls I might never see again, but they shall forever remain parts of my journey, beautiful fleeting moments of love and beauty we shared together while pink magnolias and cherries were in bloom.

Words by Steven Flynn

As a lover of all things nature it always gives me a sense of safety when I look at art and can feel that warm embrace of Mother Nature herself. The softness, the strength and the femininity of the natural world, captured within a photograph.

I feel that same embrace whenever I see any of Aks' images. The ability she has when she finds the delicate balance of composition, coupled with her use of colour is truly magical. Whether it is a portrait of her grandmother or a macro view of the flowers of a self-sown aubergine plant, I get a reflection of every woman that has passed her grandmothers eyes and a shared feeling of pride for every woman that gives a delighted smile when her nurtured plant finally begins to flower. It truly is an honour to be close enough to Aks to be able to see her work reflecting the growth she is experiencing in exploring her own womanhood.

With every image there is progression. With every image there is tenderness. And beyond everything else, there is the strength of the woman behind the camera. A true spiritual warrior.

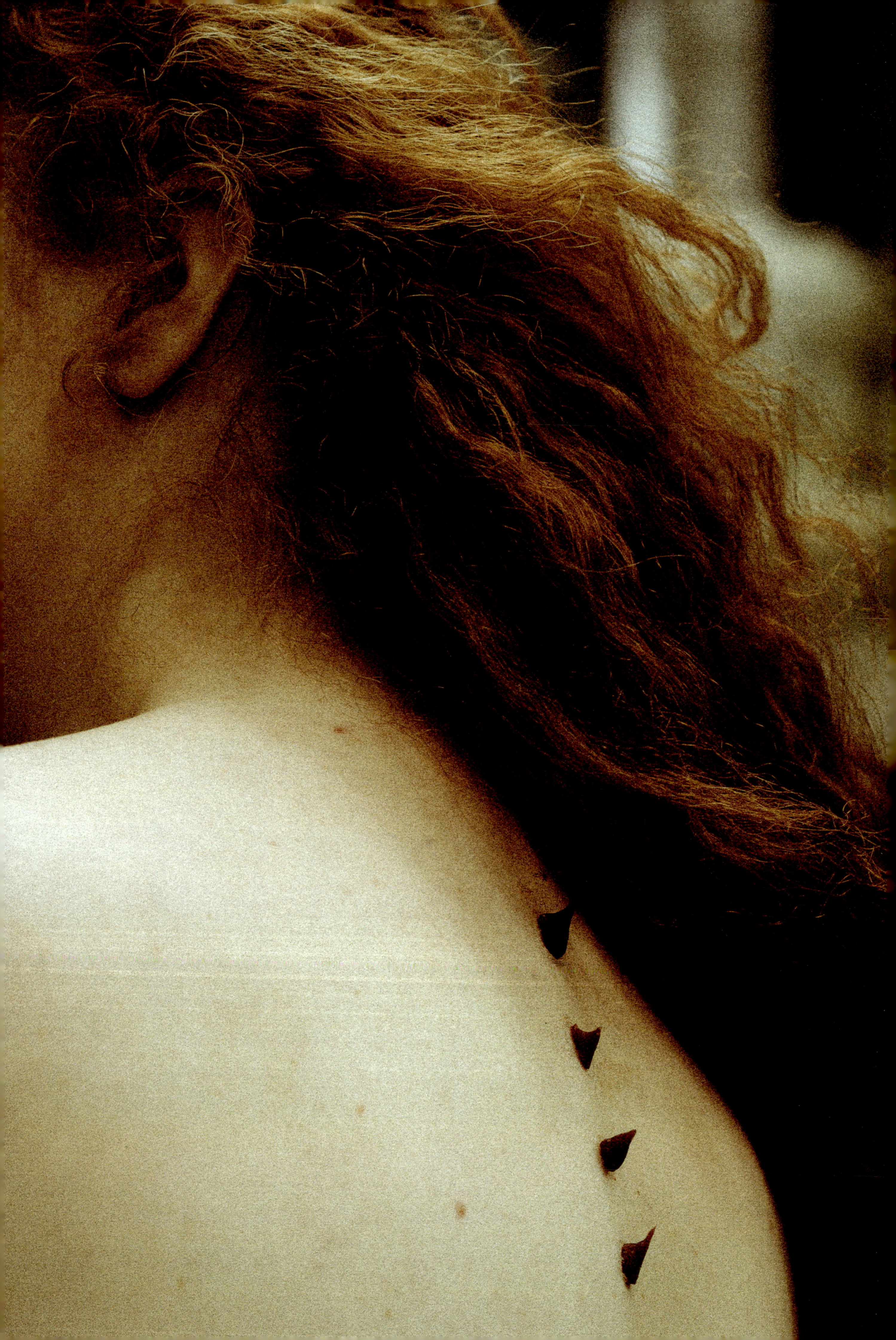

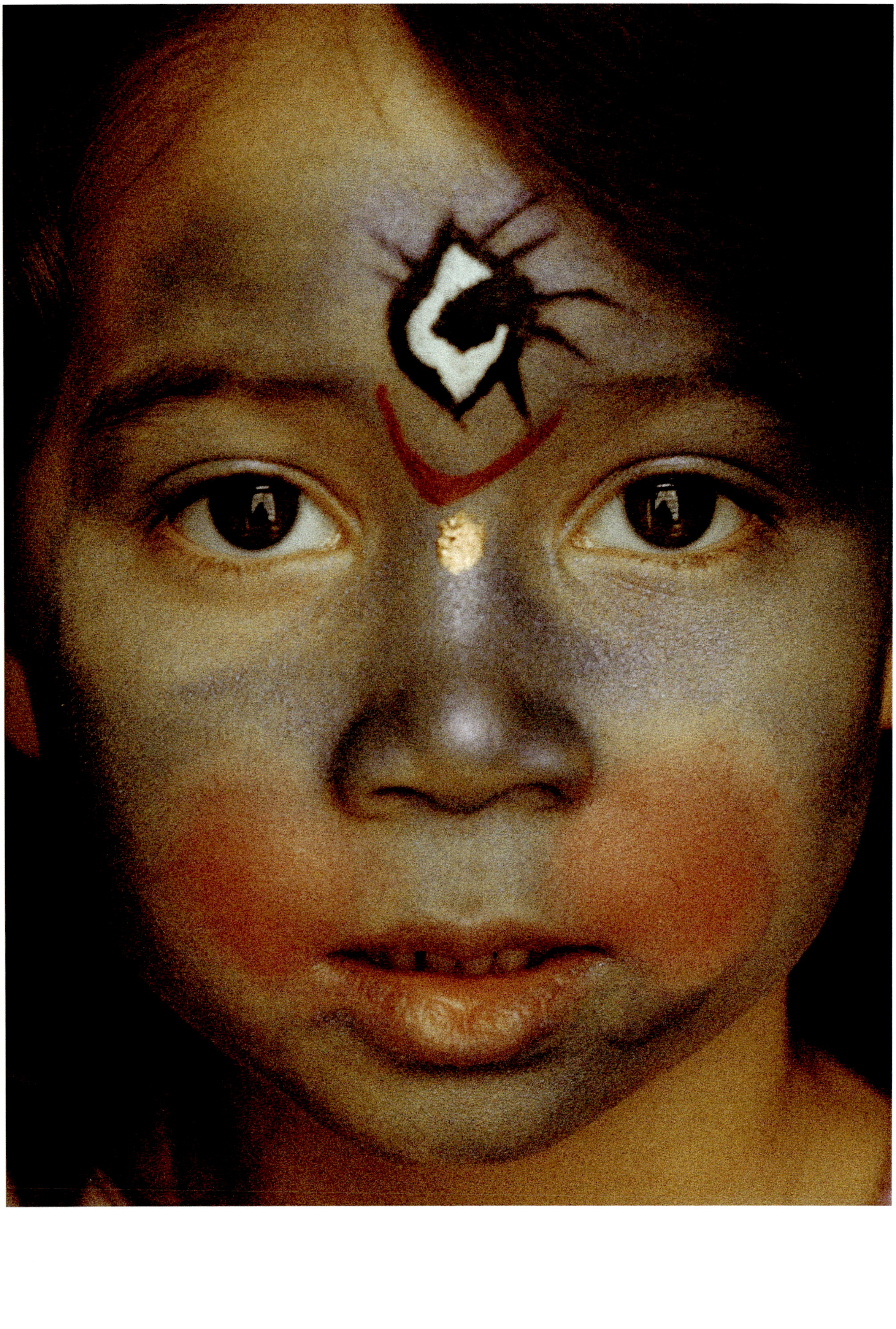

Budapest

Kodak

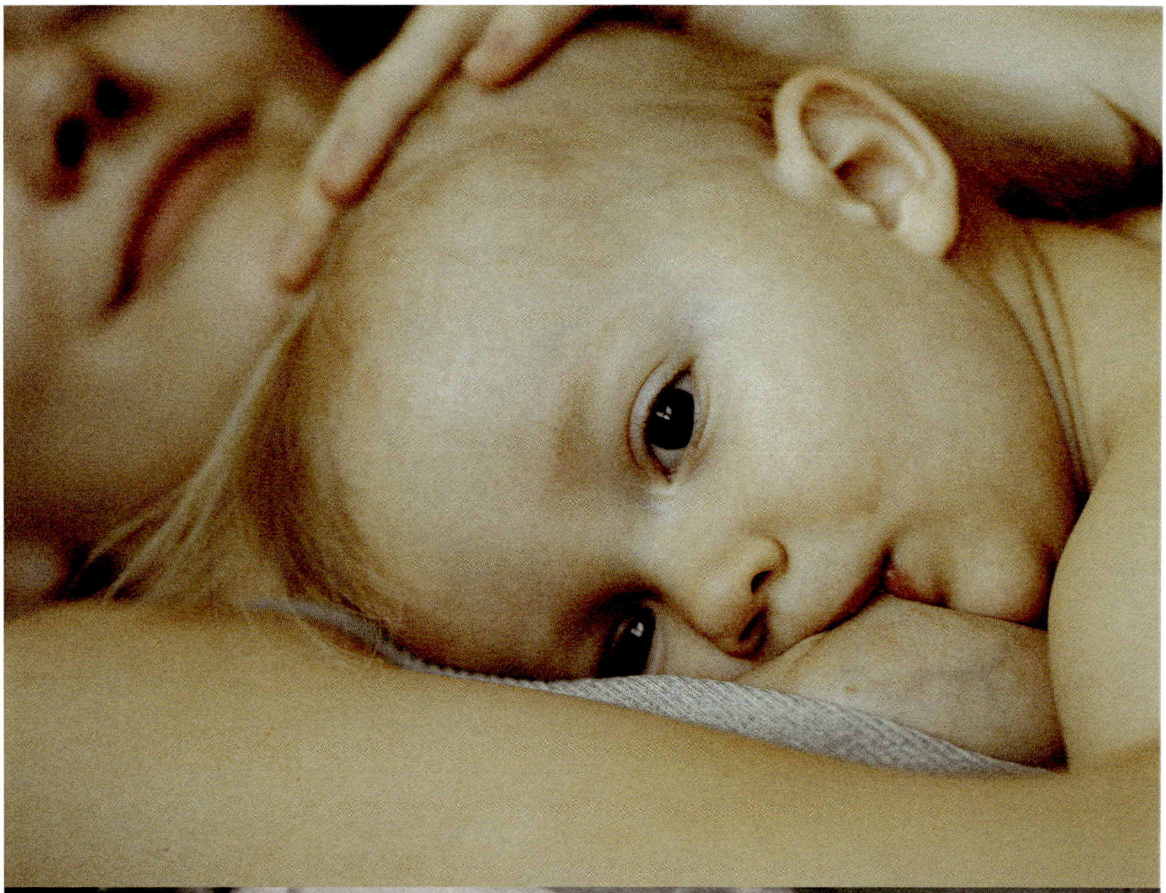

A MEAL
WITHOUT
WINE
IS CALLED
BREAKFAST

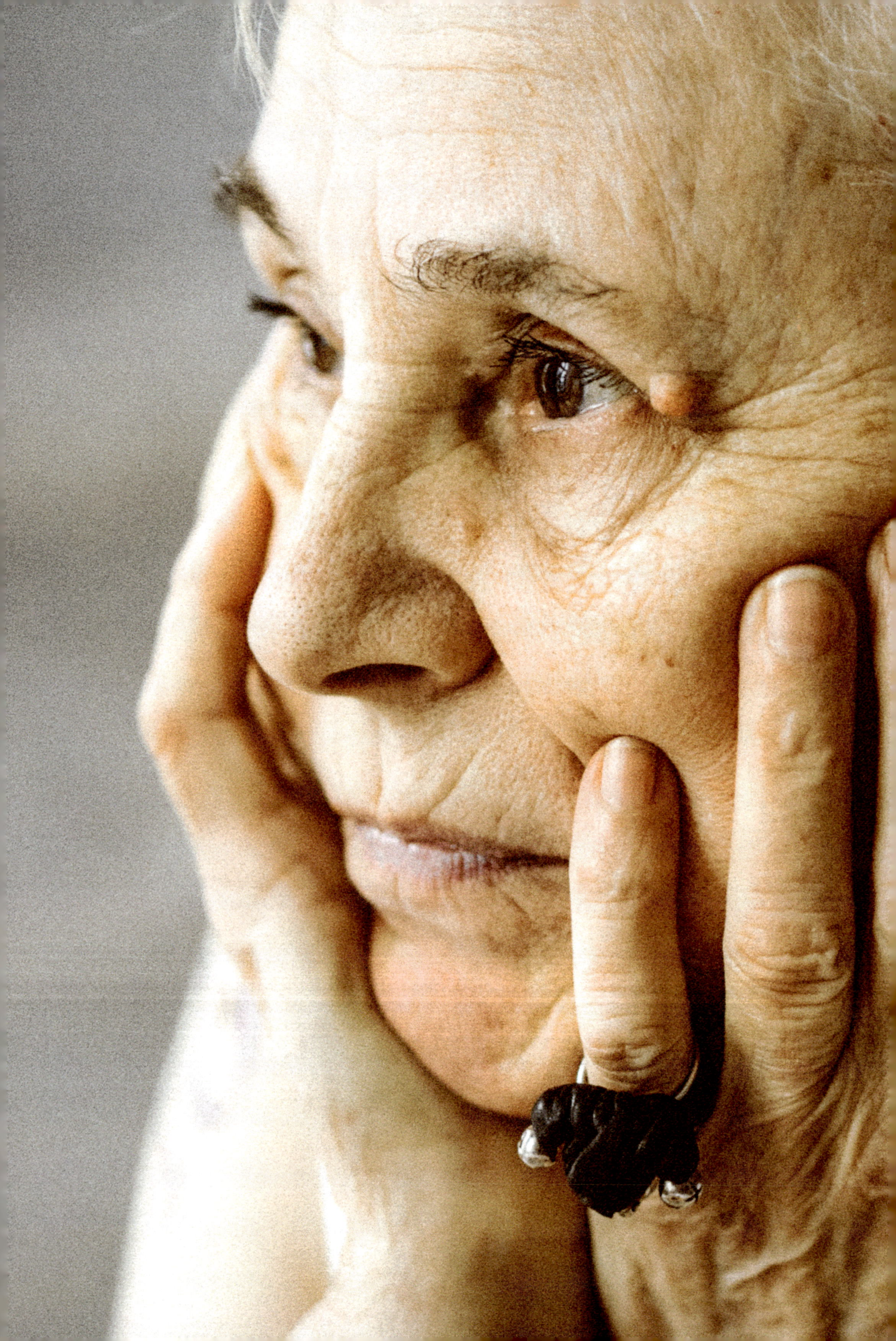

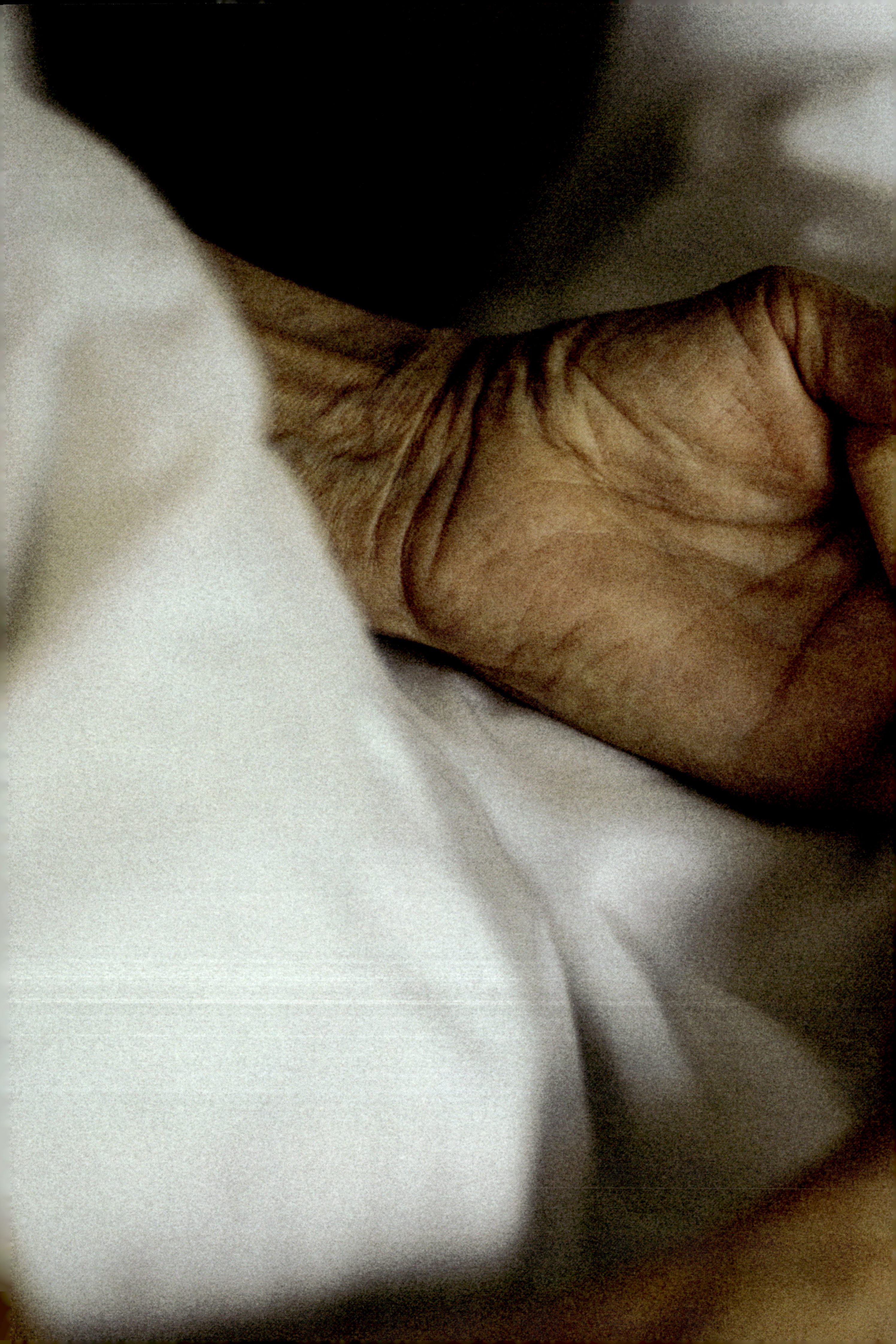

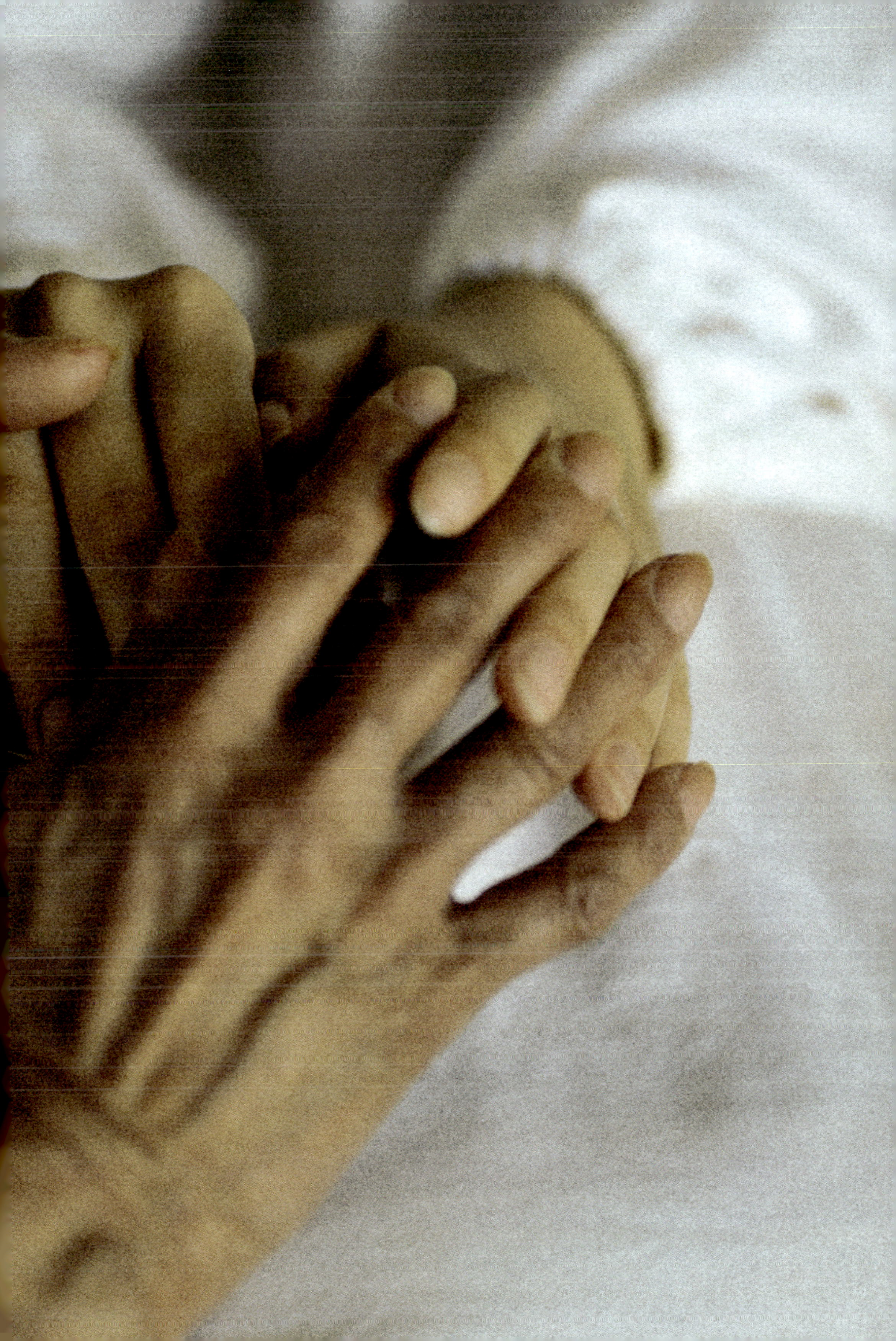

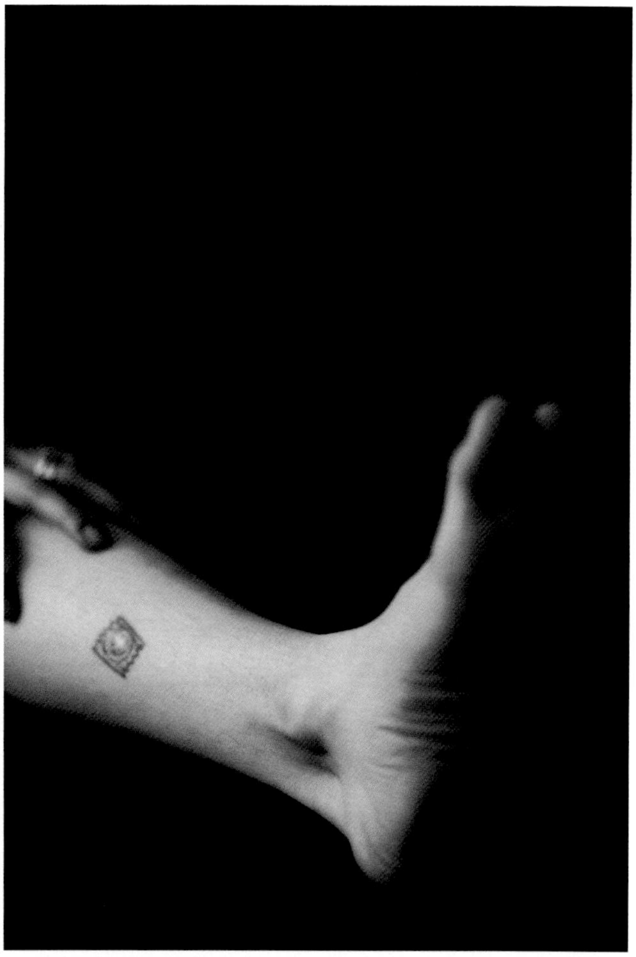

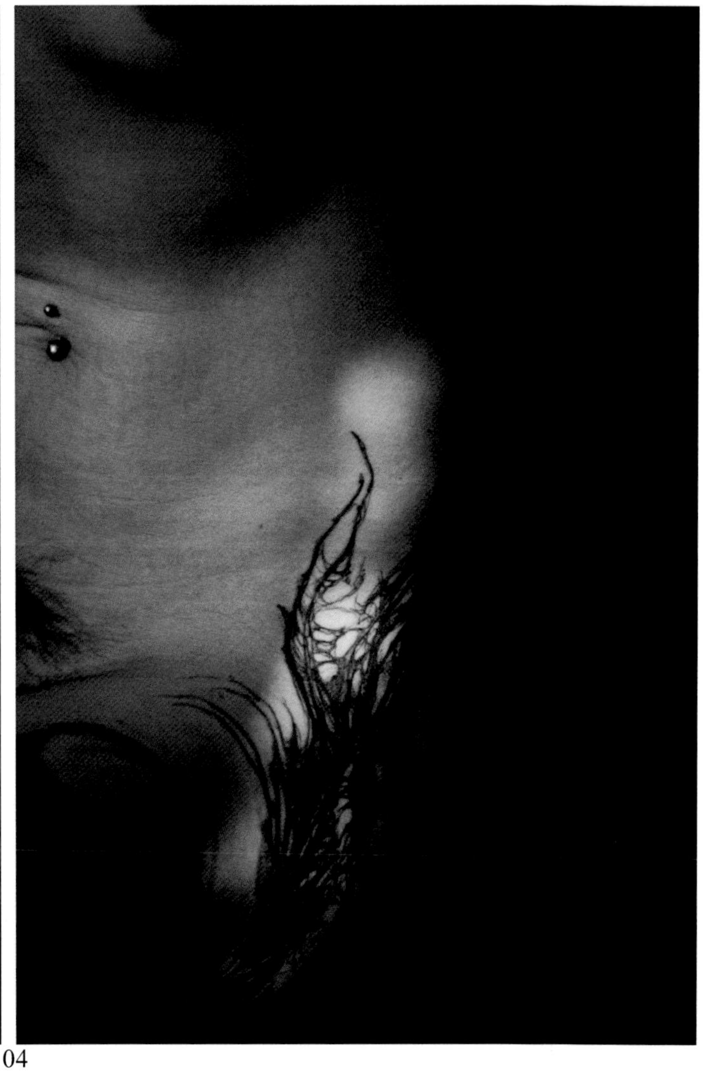

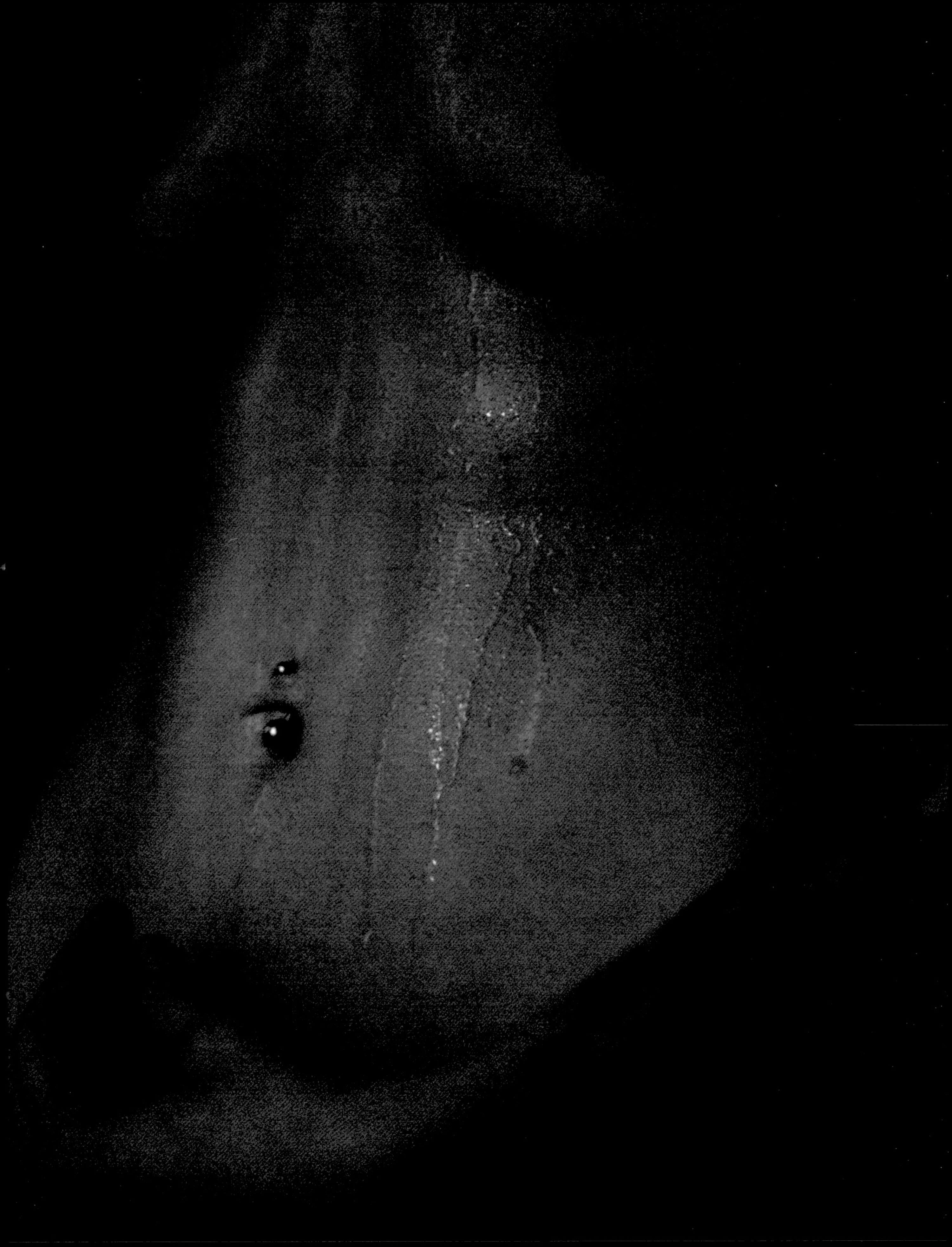

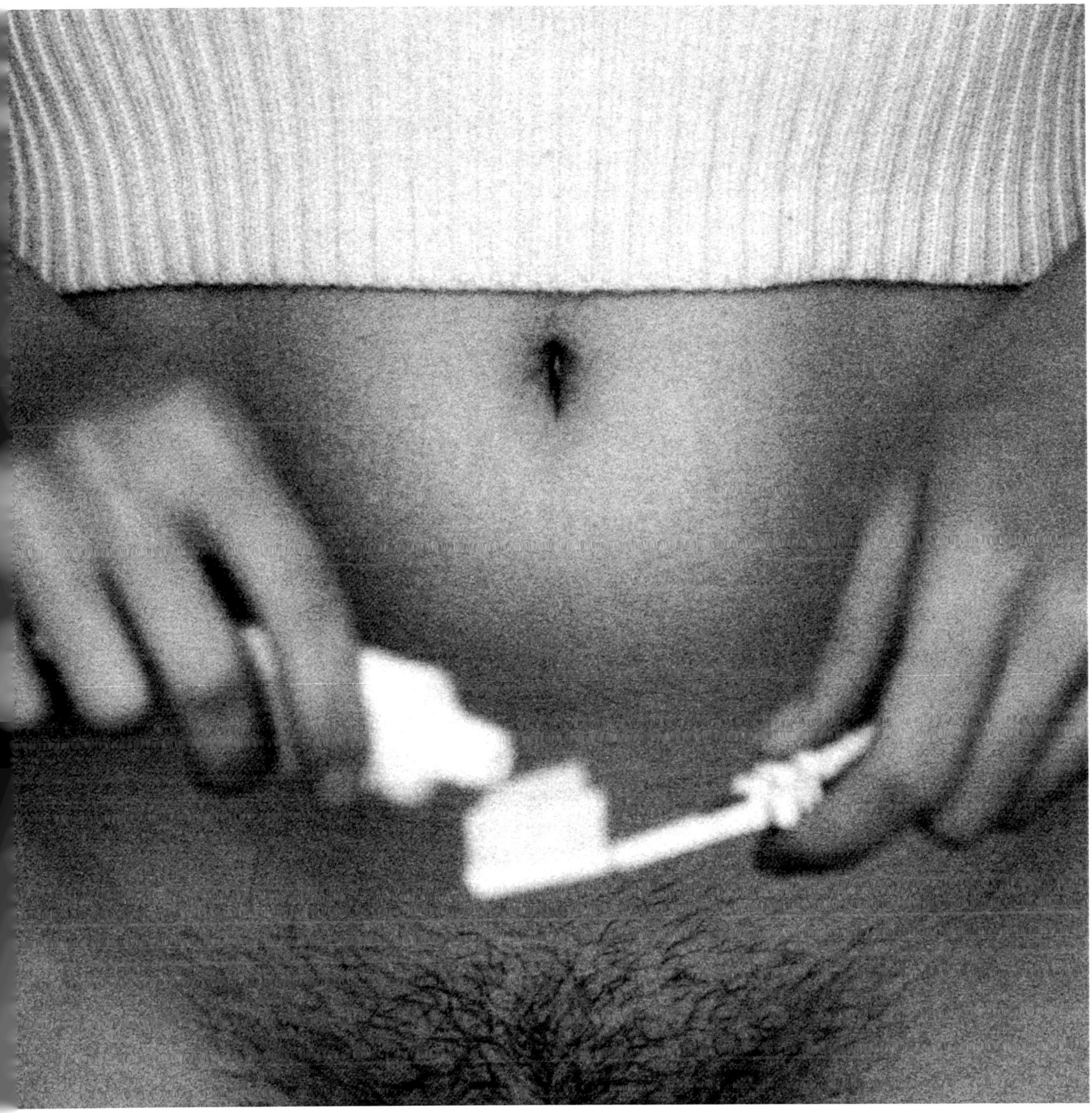

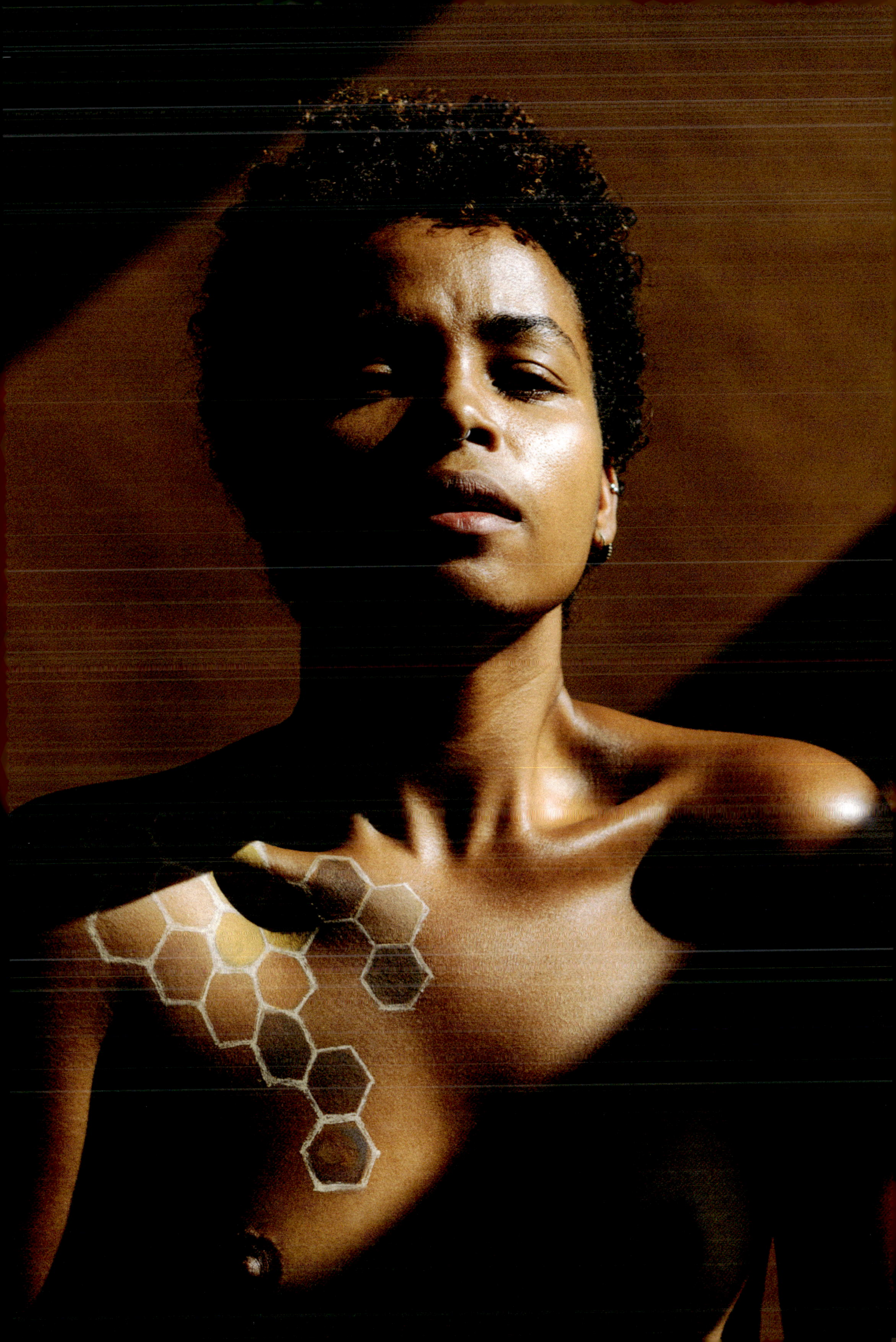

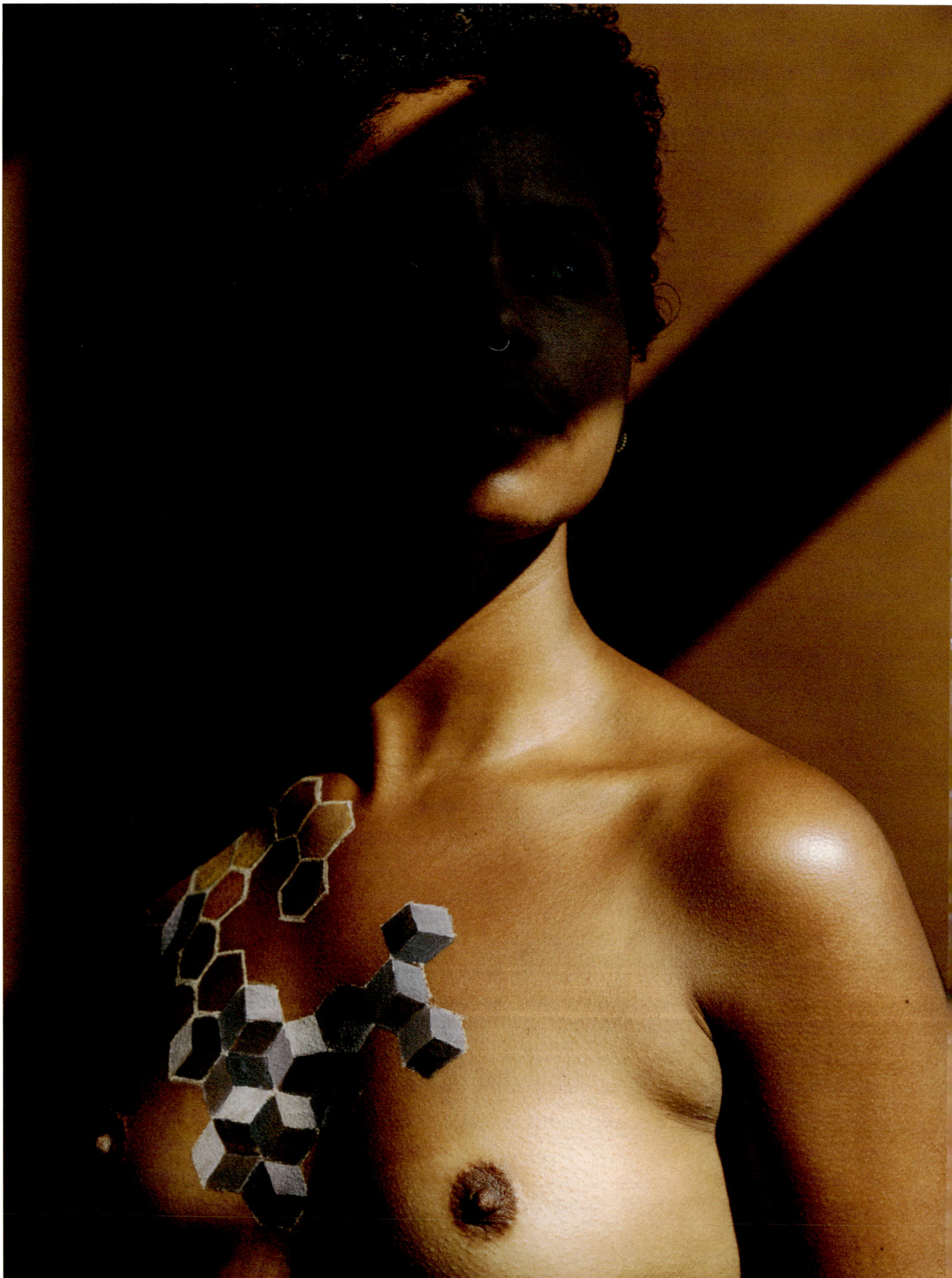

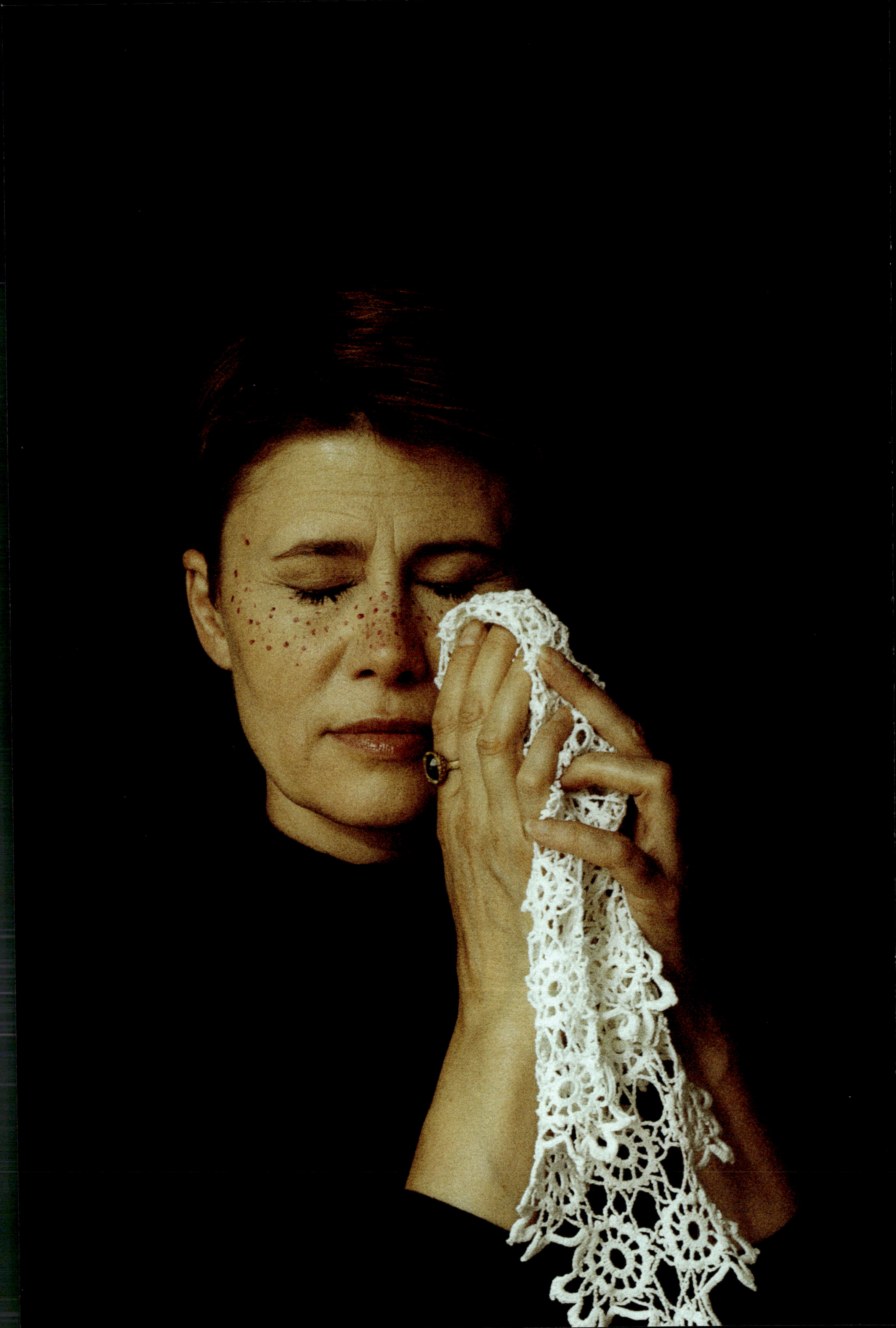

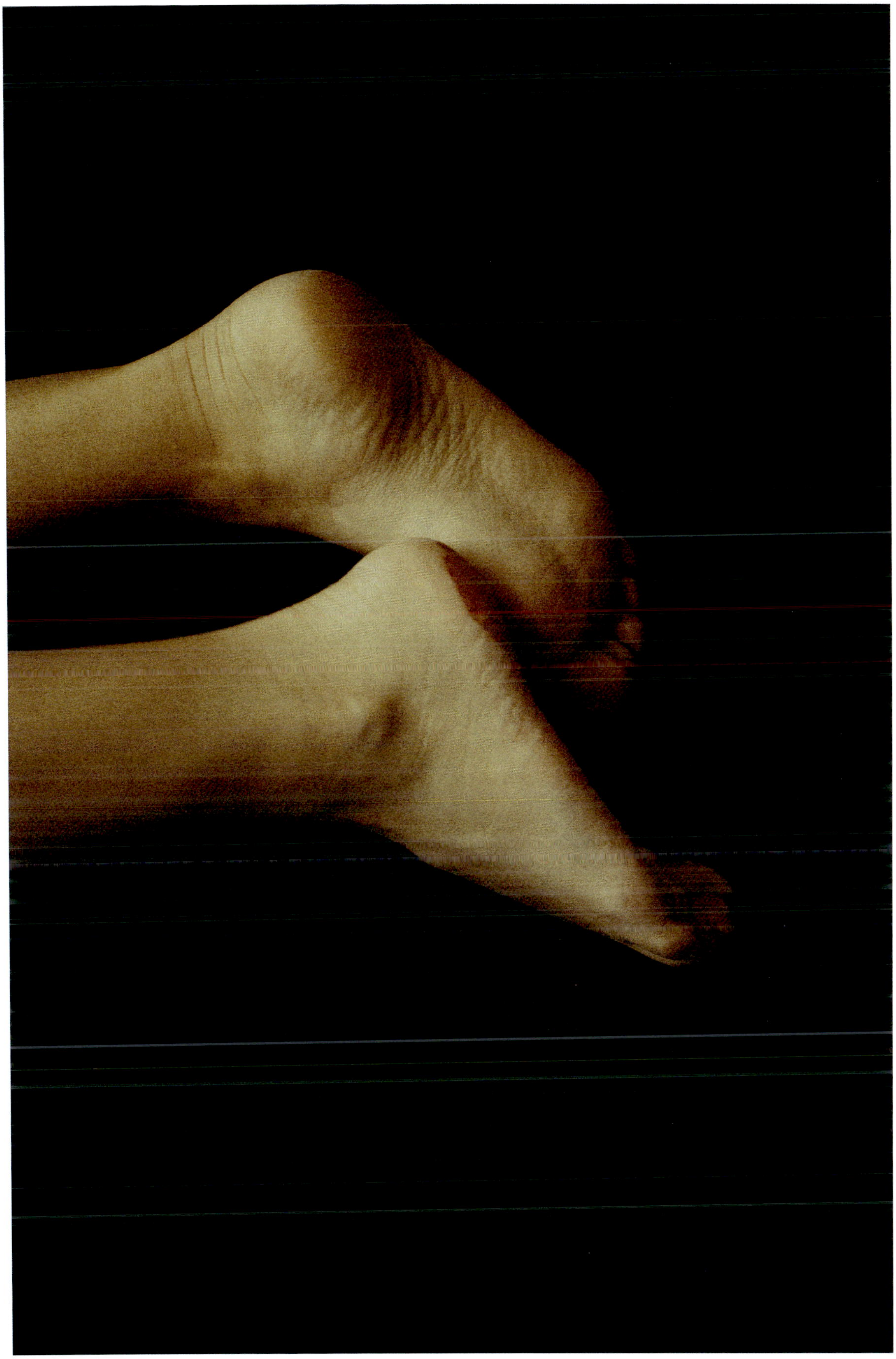

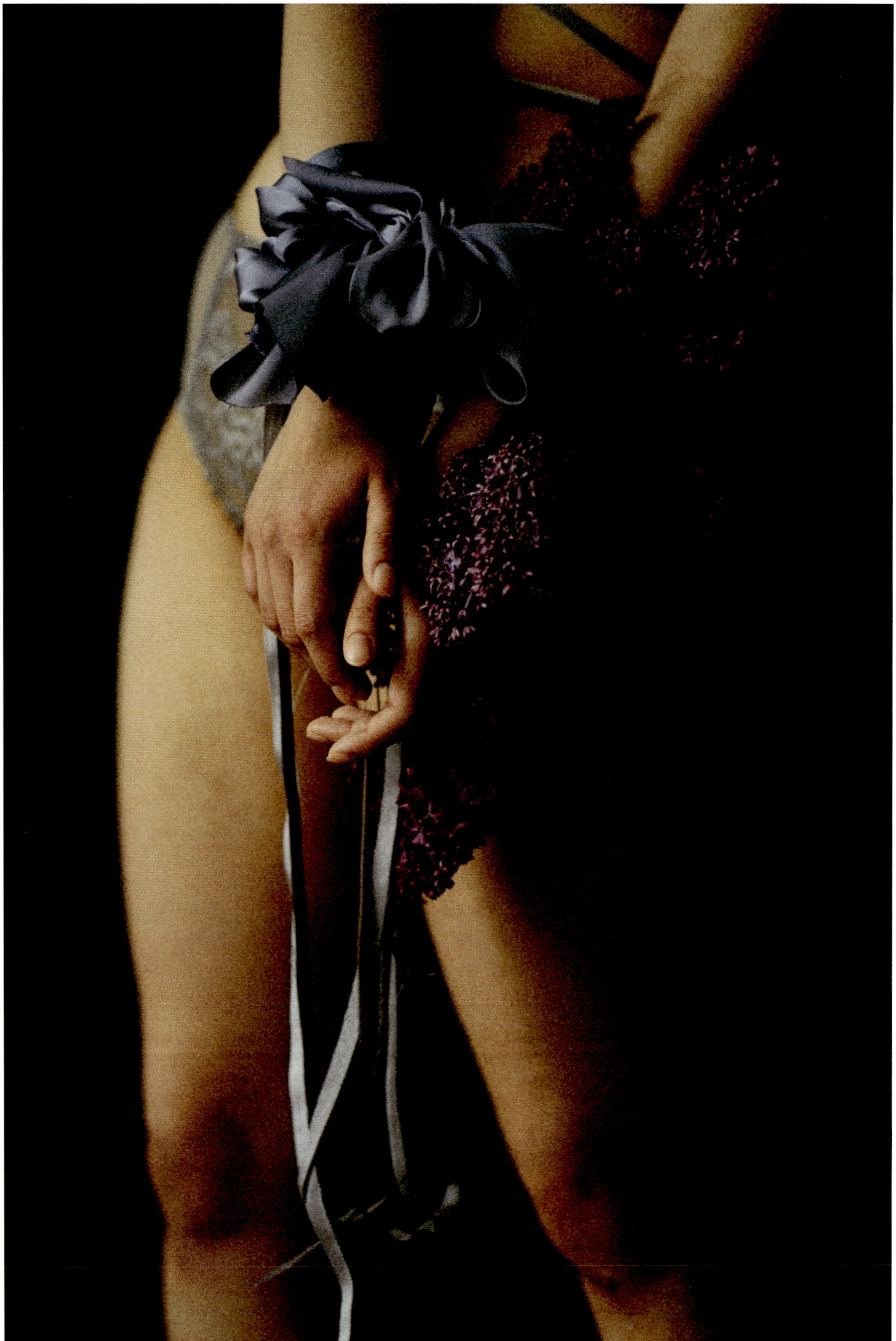

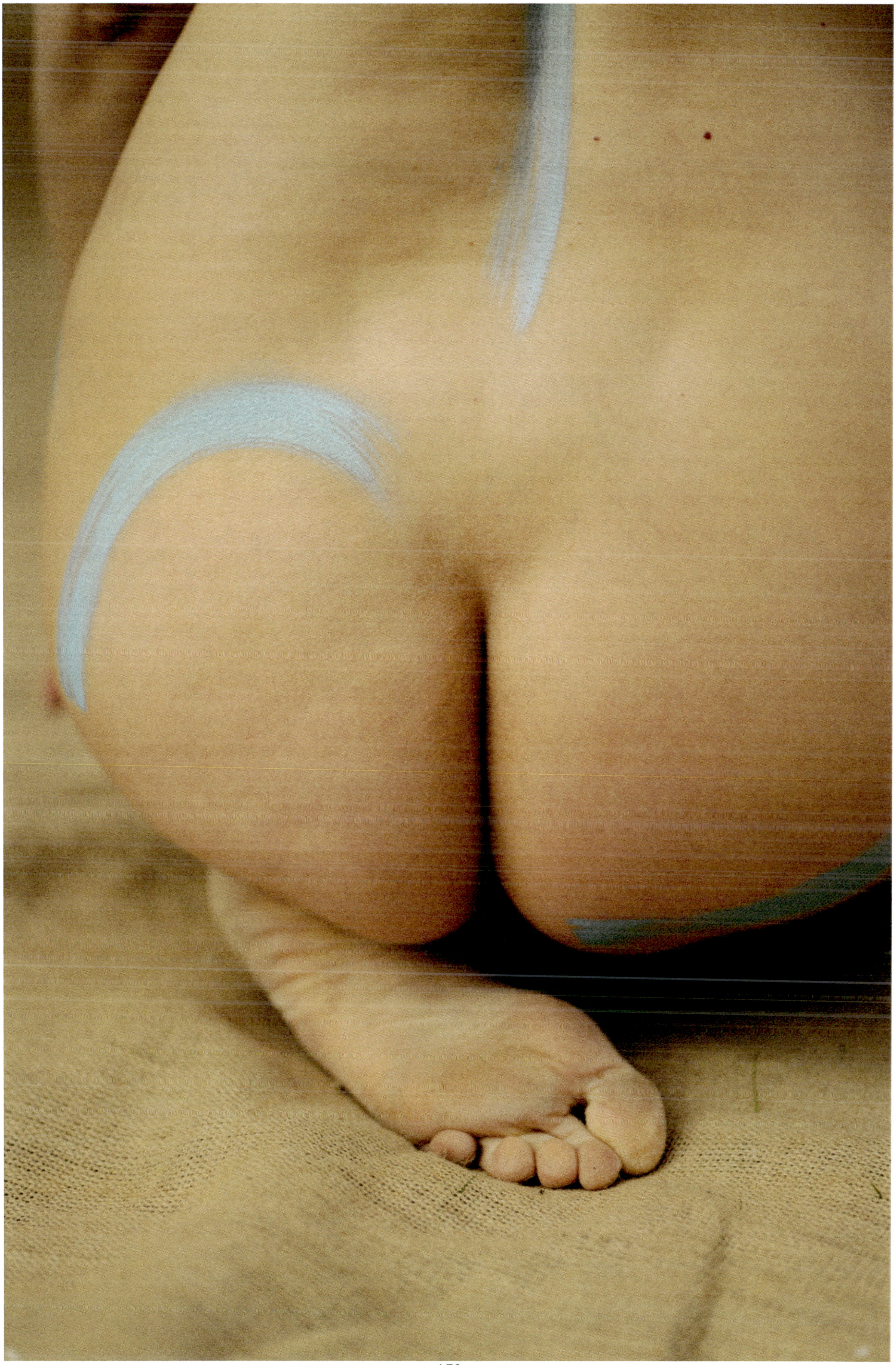

The list of photographs

Afterword by Ivan Konovalov

Perhaps, you've been wandering amongst the wooden shelves in your favourite bookshop or maybe you saw an advertisement on the internet, and your eyes caught a beautiful cover of an unknown to you author. Or perhaps, someone, who's been admiring the colour of your eyes for the past 10 minutes, gingerly came up to you, holding this book under their armpit. Now, with this serendipitous meet-cute, you've got a debutant edition of a wonderful young photographer with a mysterious name in your hands. As soon as you leave your number to this lovely stranger you just met, anticipating it to be one of the most pivotal encounters of your life, the time will come to get to know this book better.

In it, the author is attempting to open up the great versatility of a female nature with a special tenderness and a vision, that demonstrates an intense sensitivity and an irrepressible force of her heroines. Aks was born in Russia, but she lived most of her conscious life in the UK, and, as a true child of the world, she has traveled all over Europe, Asia, South America and beyond. Her endless journey helps her to sense the life path of each character in a unique way, regardless of the exact geographical location in which the picture has been taken, to display the subjects' mentality, feelings and beautiful characteristics through the prism of her lens. The diversity of their stories and that specific gentle approach to each woman during a shoot, allows her to create a friendly environment in the process. Every participant feels safe to open their heart up, maintaining the sacred nature and intimacy of this fleeting little world, that only exists while the camera is clicking, but which contains the whole universe of events and images within it.

This collection of portraits is weening to inspire you to do mad and loving deeds for your favourite creatures, to inspire you to dream and to travel, to discover the little and big worlds around you, to find your own journey.

You could also gift this book to your friend, without any special occasion or simply to express your feelings, but purely to share some beauty with someone you treasure, as that is the author's main goal – to bring as much love into this world as possible.